Samantha Smith

Journey
to the
Soviet Union

Samantha Smith

Journey to the Soviet Union

THE PEACE ABBEY
Sherborn, Massachusetts

 OCEAN TREE BOOKS
Santa Fe, New Mexico

Second Edition.

Published by:
THE PEACE ABBEY
Two North Main Street
Sherborn MA 01770
(508) 655-2143   *www.peaceabbey.org*

Available to the trade:
OCEAN TREE BOOKS
Post Office Box 1295
Santa Fe NM 87504
(505) 983-1412   *www.oceantree.com*

ISBN-13: 978-0-943734-44-6
ISBN-10: 0-943734-44-4
(Supercedes 0-316-80175-5 and 0-316-80176-3)

Library of Congress CIP Data:
Smith, Samantha
    Samantha Smith: journey to the Soviet Union
    Summary: A ten-year-old girl from Maine describes her trip to Russia at the invitation of Yuri Andropov after writing him a letter expressing her fears about nuclear war.
    1. Soviet Union—Description and travel—1970—Juvenile literature. 2. Peace—Juvenile literature.
[1. Soviet Union—Description and travel. 2. Smith, Samantha. 3. Children's writings.] I. Title.
II: Title: Journey to the Soviet Union.
DK29.S62 1985   914.7'0485   84-19436

Photographs reproduced by permission of Richard Howell/*People Weekly*, pages 2, 10, 12; Gene Willman, United Press International, 7, 11, 48; Bowdoin College Public Relations Department, 15 (top); Ron Maxwell, Waterville, Maine *Morning Sentinel*, 15 (bottom); Pat Wellenbach, The Associated Press, 18, 122; Arthur Smith, 16, 19, 23, 46, 58, 62, 70, 74, 75, 84, 94, 95. All other photos courtesy of TASS news agency.

An Ocean Tree Peacewatch Edition
Printed in the United States of America.

I dedicate this book to the children of the world.
They know that peace is always possible.

Many people helped to make this book possible. I especially want to thank my Mom and Dad for helping with my grammar and all the details of writing. At Little, Brown and Company in Boston, Betsy Isele and Bob Lowe sorted out the pictures and organized and designed the book. I must give special thanks to Dr. Lee Salk for his encouragement. And I want to thank the excellent photographers of TASS, Associated Press, and United Press International, who traveled with me on this journey.

O wonder!
How many goodly creatures are there here!
How beauteous mankind is! O brave new world
That has such people in't!

—Miranda
in *The Tempest*

Seeing the world through the eyes of children can renew our contact with nature and with some of the most important elements in life. Children have a natural curiosity, and their questions are painfully direct, open, and honest. Because their minds have not yet been contaminated by social and political constraints, we find that children everywhere ask the same questions: "How does life begin?" "Where does the sky end?" "Why do grown-ups make wars?"

As long as children ask challenging questions and grown-ups respond to those questions, there will be hope for humankind.

It was a child's question and her responsive parents that launched a fairy-tale-like voyage bringing children together in an atmosphere of love, respect and joy, which warmed the hearts of millions of people around the world and left ambassadors, diplomats and politicians scratching their heads in bewilderment.

The voyage of Samantha Smith is precisely that – a trip to a foreign land at a time of great world tension, which brought together people who realized how much they are alike.

Samantha Smith has become a symbol of hope to all children. Her simple question, supported by loving parents, led to greater human understanding, and has shown us the power of a child in lessening the tensions between two world powers.

Perhaps we should cease asking children "Why don't you act like a grown-up"" and begin asking adults "Why don't you think like a child?"

Lee Salk
Sandbar Island
Rockwood, Maine
August 1984

THE PEACE LITERATURE PROJECT

Inspired by the students of the Life Experience School, the Peace Literature Project in Honor of Samantha Smith has been created by The Peace Abbey to educate students about peace and promote peace literature for school-age children. It is the dream of the Peace Literature Project that some day every American school and town will have a section of its library devoted entirely to peace so that children like Sierra, Olivia, Jackson, Nathaniel, Noah, and thousands of others may learn that, like Samantha, one person with courage and determination can change attitudes and help to create a more peaceful world.

INTRODUCTION

A Girl Who Made a Difference

Samantha Smith was a young American girl who asked a simple question and changed the attitudes of two great nations.

In the 1980s, the United States and the Soviet Union were still in the grip of a Cold War – a struggle between Western democracy and communism as systems of government. Each country threatened the other with destruction by nuclear weapons, and each kept making more and more of them. Ten-year-old Samantha Smith worried about war and dreamed of peace. So she wrote a letter to Yuri Andropov, the new leader of the Soviet Union: "Dear Mr. Andropov," she wrote, "I have been worrying about Russia and the United States getting into a nuclear war. Are you going to vote to have a have a war or not?"

He did not answer right away, but a few months later there was a phone call waiting for her at the principal's office at her school in Manchester, Maine. And so began her amazing journey. . .

Samantha's journey to the Soviet Union came to symbolize peace between the two nations. She proved that one person can make a real difference. Her courage, faith, and determination to make a positive change in the world made her a hero for all ages.

After returning to America, she was invited to appear on television often. She was host of a Disney Channel special educating kids abut the candidates in the 1984 presidential campaign, she spoke at an international children's conference in Japan, she starred in the *Lime Street* television series.

And she wrote this book.

Sadly, on August 25, 1985, Samantha and her father were killed in a plane crash. They were on their way home from London where she had finished filming a segment for the TV series. She was then 13 years old. Around the world, people remembered the inspiring girl and her famous trip. At least one school in America is named for Samantha and in Russia there were many memorials including a postage stamp in honor of their young American friend.

Among those attending Samantha's funeral service were the children of the Peace Abbey's Life Experience School from Sherborn, Massachusetts. At the Life Experience School, children with severe life challenges learn to value altruism and service to others. In their peace studies, these young people learn the importance of compassion and nonviolence.

People magazine took pictures of my family on our back steps.

Actually, the whole thing started when I asked my mother if there was was going to be a war. There was always something on television about missiles and nuclear bombs. Once I watched a science show on public television and the scientists said that a nuclear war would wreck the Earth and destroy our atmosphere. Nobody could win a nuclear war. I remembered that I woke up one morning and wondered if this was going to be the last day of the Earth.

I asked my mother who would start a war and why. She showed me a newsmagazine with a story about America and Russia, one that had a picture of the new Russian leader, Yuri Andropov, on the cover. We read it together. It seemed that the people in both Russia and America were worried that the other country would start a nuclear war. It all seemed so dumb to me. I had learned about the awful things

3

that had happened during World War II, so I thought that nobody would ever want to have another war. I told Mom that she should write to Mr. Andropov to find out who was causing all the trouble. She said, "Why don't *you* write to him?" So I did.

Dear Mr. Andropov,

My name is Samantha Smith. I am ten years old. Congratulations on your new job. I have been worrying about Russia and the United States getting into a nuclear war. Are you going to vote to have a war or not? If you aren't please tell me how you are going to help to not have a war. This question you do not have to answer, but I would like to know why you want to conquer the world or at least our country. God made the world for us to live together in peace and not to fight.

Sincerely,
Samantha Smith

I wrote in my most careful handwriting since I am not always so neat. I didn't want him to have any trouble reading the letter. My mother helped me with the address:

> *Mr. Yuri Andropov*
> *The Kremlin*
> *Moscow*
> *USSR*

And my dad mailed the letter. The stamp cost 40¢ because the letter had so far to go.

Four or five months went by and nothing happened. Just when I had pretty much forgotten about the letter, Mrs. Peabody, the Manchester Elementary School secretary, called me into the office at school for a telephone call. It was a reporter from the United Press International. The reporter wanted to know if I had really written a letter to Yuri Andropov. The Russian newspaper, *Pravda*, had written an article about my letter, and they had even printed a picture of it. She said she didn't know if Mr. Andropov was going to write back to me.

My dad got a copy of *Pravda* and found some Russian teachers to help translate the article. The article did not answer the questions I had asked, but it did say I could be excused for misunderstanding because I was only ten years old. And it never said anything about why Mr. Andropov didn't answer my letter.

So I decided to write another letter to try to find out what was going on. This time I wrote to Ambassador Dobrynin. He's the head of the USSR Embassy in Washington, D.C. I asked the ambassador if Mr. Andropov would answer my questions, and I also said I thought my questions were good ones and it shouldn't matter if I was ten years old.

About a week later I had a telephone call from a man with a heavy accent. The caller said that he was from the Soviet Union, and he said that I would soon be getting a letter from Yuri Andropov, the General Secretary of the Central Committee of the Communist Party of the USSR. The man on the phone sounded like someone in a movie. I thought maybe this was one of Dad's friends playing a joke. He wanted me to call back when the letter came, and he gave me a bunch of telephone numbers to write down. Later, my dad checked the numbers and they were from the embassy of the USSR!

A few days later, Alice, the postmistress, called from the post office to say that a special envelope had arrived for me. We rushed to the post office, and Dad and I read the letter on the way to school.

Samantha Smith
Manchester, Maine
USA

Dear Samantha,

I received your letter, which is like many others that have reached me recently from your country and from other countries around the world.

It seems to me—I can tell by your letter—that you are a courageous and honest girl, resembling Becky, the friend of Tom Sawyer in the famous book of your compatriot Mark Twain. This book is well known and loved in our country by all boys and girls.

You write that you are anxious about whether there will be a nuclear war between our two countries. And you ask are we doing anything so that war will not break out.

Your question is the most important of those that every thinking man can pose. I will reply to you seriously and honestly.

Yes, Samantha, we in the Soviet Union are trying to do everything so that there will not be war between our countries, so that in general there will not be war on earth. This is

The letter from Mr. Andropov.

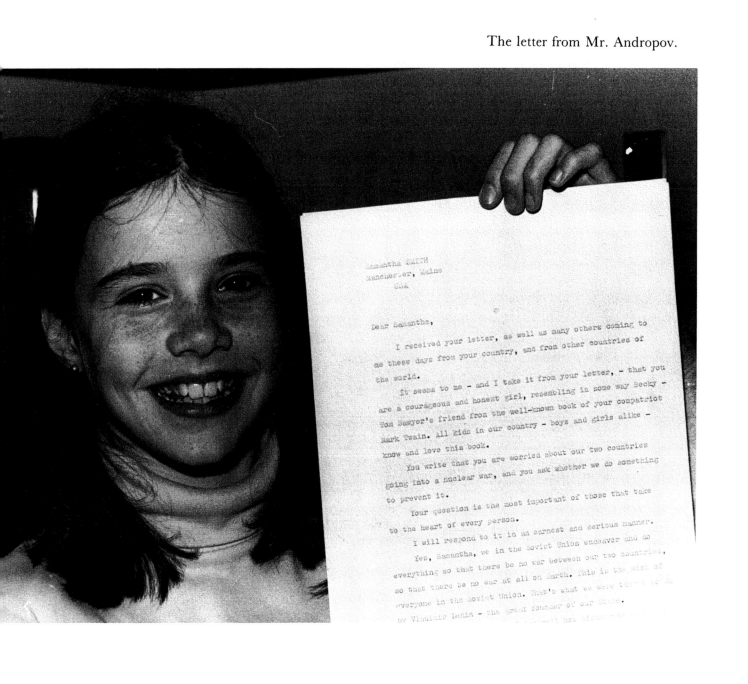

what every Soviet man wants. This is what the great founder of our state, Vladimir Lenin, taught us.

Soviet people well know what a terrible thing war is. Forty-two years ago, Nazi Germany, which strived for supremacy over the whole world, attacked our country, burned and destroyed many thousands of our towns and villages, killed millions of Soviet men, women and children.

In that war, which ended with our victory, we were in alliance with the United States: together we fought for the liberation of many people from the Nazi invaders. I hope that you know about this from your history lessons in school. And today we want very much to live in peace, to trade and cooperate with all our neighbors on this earth—with those far away and those near by. And certainly with such a great country as the United States of America.

In America and in our country there are nuclear weapons— terrible weapons that can kill millions of people in an instant. But we do not want them ever to be used. That's precisely why the Soviet Union solemnly declared throughout the entire world that never—never—will it use nuclear weapons first against any country. In general we propose to discontinue further production of them and to proceed to the abolition of all the stockpiles on earth.

It seems to me that this is a sufficient answer to your second question: "Why do you want to wage war against the whole world or at least the United States?" We want nothing of the kind. No one in our country—neither workers, peasants, writers nor doctors, neither grown-ups nor children, nor members of the government—wants either a big or "little" war.

We want peace—there is something that we are occupied with: growing wheat, building and inventing, writing books and flying into space. We want peace for ourselves and for all peoples of the planet. For our children and for you, Samantha.

I invite you, if your parents will let you, to come to our country, the best time being the summer. You will find out about our country, meet with your contemporaries, visit an international children's camp—"Artek"—on the sea. And see for yourself: in the Soviet Union—everyone is for peace and friendship among peoples.

Thank you for your letter. I wish you all the best in your young life.

Y. Andropov

Mr. Andropov wanted me to visit the Soviet Union! I asked Dad if we could go and he said, "We'll see." He always says that before saying yes. I just knew we were going to Russia.

When I got off the school bus at our house in the afternoon, there were reporters and TV cameramen all over the front yard. This all seemed kind of silly, but it was fun. The silliest part was that everyone asked the same questions over and over: "Why did you write to Mr. Andropov?" "Did you expect Mr. Andropov to answer your letter?" "Will you go to the USSR?" "What do you think of all this?"

The first time I saw myself on television, tears came to my eyes. I wasn't afraid or anything like that, but it was a weird feeling. The reporters kept asking if I was nervous about all this, which I wasn't, but I wondered if I was *supposed* to be nervous.

Then the TV and radio news shows started calling from all over the world—London, and Japan, and

My friend Lynn D'Avanzo gave me moral support at the table while I was interviewed.

Australia, and other faraway places. CBS and NBC sent a chartered plane up to Maine just to fly Mom and me down to New York City and I went on the *CBS Morning News* and the *Today Show* and *Nightline*. The best part was when Tara from *Nightline* had a limousine and driver show us around the city, and we saw the Statue of Liberty, the Bronx Zoo, and a lot of other famous places I had never seen. Then we had a fancy dinner and went to see *Porgy and Bess* on Broadway, but I fell asleep during the show because I was so tired.

It's a funny feeling to see articles about yourself with pictures in a newspaper you can't read.

Mr. Alexander Druzhinin of Soviet TV and his cameraman came to our house to talk to me. And United States press people came to our house to talk to *him*. It was a little crowded in our living room with all those cameras and microphones.

When we got home the next day, there were even more reporters because a Soviet TV crew came all the way from Washington to Manchester. Now the American TV crews wanted to film the Soviet crew talking to me. One photographer even came all the way from Paris.

There were hundreds of letters, which Dad was trying to answer. Dad had just finished teaching at the university, but Mom still had a regular workday at the Maine Department of Human Services. I think Dad gave up when the letter pile got to be over a thousand. Johnny Carson invited us to California to be on his TV show. My best friend, Lynn, got permission from her mother to go with me and Mom, which made the trip even more fun. Lynn and I really wanted to see what California would be like. It was a super trip and Johnny Carson was very nice even if he did kiss me. In California, everybody shakes your hand and then kisses you. Dad stayed home to answer the telephone, which rang about every two minutes all day long.

When we flew back from New York to meet the Soviet TV people, an unexpected crowd of reporters met us at the airport in Augusta.

After we got back from California, I had to finish the fifth grade and start practice with my softball team. I played catcher or shortstop on the team and that spring we had a great season. When I tried real hard to hit a home run, I could never do it. Then, when I didn't think much about it—*blam!*—I could hit a homer with the bases loaded. It's hard to relax when everybody is yelling like crazy.

We decided to go to Russia in July. We had a lot of planning to do, and Nonnie, my grandmother, and my cousin Tyler came up to help us get ready. They were going to stay at our house and take care of everything including the cats and my Chesapeake Bay retriever, Kim.

My parents decided that it would be good to go to Russia because it would help us all think about what our two countries were really arguing about. We were going to leave on July 7 and stay for two weeks.

I found travel books about Russia at the library. Actually, Russia should be called the Soviet Union and the people should be called Soviets because there are many parts of the country that are not Russian. In the library books it all looked beautiful and very different from life in Maine.

Lots of questions came into my head when I looked at pictures of Soviet people. I wondered if I could be friends with Soviet kids. Would they think that I was a spy or that I was afraid of them? Would they think that I wanted to conquer them? Maybe they would hate me. Some kids had written letters to me saying that they thought I was very brave to write that letter. Well, writing the letter didn't take any bravery, but I would have to be brave if the Soviet kids didn't like me.

Our trip to the Soviet Union began at the airport

Maine colleges helped provide us
with gifts for our hosts in the Soviet
Union.

The press conference at Montreal airport

in Augusta, Maine. A bunch of reporters and photographers waited with us at the airport, but I knew most of them by now so it was like having more friends to say goodbye to. When we got to Boston there was a huge crowd of reporters and cameramen and the state police made them all keep back until we could get to the press conference room at Logan Airport. Then the state police took us to a private room where we could relax for a while, and finally we flew to Montreal.

Reporters in Montreal seemed to go wild and even the Royal Canadian Mounted Police, who were trying to guide us, had trouble holding back the people when the reporters started shoving. It was ridiculous. They were all pushing microphones at me and shouting and then we all got jammed up and I bit one of the microphones that was pushed up against my face. When I thought about it later on, it was very funny. If the reporters would just stand still and raise their hands—then maybe nobody would panic. But I guess it wouldn't seem so exciting, either.

We're off
to Boston.

On the jet from Boston
to Montreal

Our Soviet airliner flew for nine hours, all the way from Montreal to Moscow without stopping. When we landed at Sheremetjevo Airport in Moscow, it was crowded and noisy with reporters. Reporters were there from America and Europe and Moscow, and I couldn't see because there were so many bright camera lights. I was tired from jet lag and the reporters wanted to know what I thought about Moscow. How could I answer that when I just walked off the airplane? Actually, it was exciting to think that this really was the Soviet Union. But I didn't have enough time to think up something to say to the reporters—it's hard to think when everybody is shouting questions.

We were met at the airport by our guides for the two-week visit, Gennady Fedosov and Natasha Semenikhina. They drove us to the Hotel Sovietskaya, which was very beautiful and looked like a palace.

21

The man next to me is from the
Soviet Friendship Society.

There was even a piano in one of our rooms and the cooks at the hotel sent up a fancy cake and bowls of fruit and some other stuff, but I was too exhausted to eat. Mom and I played "Chopsticks" and "Heart and Soul" together on the piano and then I fell asleep. When I woke up, I couldn't remember where I was at first, and then I knew it was Moscow and it seemed like I was still dreaming. But it wasn't a dream.

That night we had dinner in a huge dining room and the waiters wore starchy white jackets. If anybody even looked at the waiters, they would rush over to see what we needed, so I had to be careful not to look anywhere near them. I ordered Chicken Kiev, which is a chicken breast cooked with hot butter in the center, and Natasha showed me how to cut it so the butter wouldn't squirt you in the eye.

At Sovietskaya Hotel, Moscow.

In Red Square. The Lenin Mauso-
leum is in the background.

Looking across Red Square toward
Kremlin Wall and Savior Gate and
Tower in the center. St. Basil's is
on the left.

Natasha has a daughter a little older than me, so she knew all about kids. For the rest of the trip I ordered Chicken Kiev if it was on the menu.

The next morning we had a meeting with Madame Zinaida Krouglova to learn about all the places we would visit in Moscow. She's the head of all the Friendship Societies between the Soviet Union and other countries, and she's also on the Central Committee of the Communist Party. When she hugs you it's like your ribs are going to crack. While we were there in Madame Krouglova's office, I had a phone call from Valentina Tereshkova, the first woman cosmonaut (the Soviets use the word *cosmonaut* instead of *astronaut*). She kept saying, "I kiss you, Samantha! I kiss you, Samantha!" She was inviting us to tea next week at her office. Valentina Tereshkova went into space almost twenty years ago, and she is now the director of the Soviet Women's Committee, which is a very important job in the Soviet Union.

In the afternoon we rode over to Red Square. Police cars led the way and we roared down the middle of the streets. We went so fast that a few times I thought we were going to crash.

Red Square is huge. We went into Lenin's Tomb, which is a dark place and kind of scary. Lenin's body lies in a lighted glass case, and we could look at the body as we walked past. It was the first time I ever saw someone who had died. Special soldiers in blue uniforms stood on guard in the tomb. Dad carried a big basket of flowers, and the chief of the

In front of Yuri Gargarin's tomb.
He was the first cosmonaut.

28

guards led the way. Lenin was the leader of the Russian Revolution in 1917, when the Bolsheviks overthrew the tsar. The Soviets have a lot of respect for Lenin and his ideas about government.

Then, we took more flowers over to Yuri Gargarin's tomb and to the Tomb of the Unknown Soldier. Yuri Gargarin was the first man in space and he is buried in the Kremlin Wall near the place where John Reed is buried. John Reed was an American who wrote about the 1917 Revolution in a book called *Ten Days That Shook the World*.

Behind the Kremlin Wall, we walked through most of the old churches and palaces of the Kremlin. These buildings are really ancient and full of religious paintings, called icons, and golden treasures. The word *Kremlin* means "fortress." Nowadays people refer to the walled-in area of old Moscow as "The Kremlin." There are also many important government buildings in this section of the city. We walked over to the building of the Supreme Soviet, which is something like our legislature, and then down to see the gigantic chandeliers in the Great Kremlin Palace. Each chandelier is nearly as big as our whole living room! Later, our Leningrad Intourist guide, Helen, told me the secret of finding out if there is real crystal in a chandelier: standing right underneath the chandelier, look up at it and roll your head in a circle twenty times. If you feel dizzy, it's because you are standing under real crystal. I'm not sure I believe that.

Gilded domes of the Upper Church
of the Savior inside the Kremlin.

In Red Square. The Museum of History is in the background.

We laid flowers on the Tomb of the Unknown Soldier adjacent to the Kremlin.

Inside the Kremlin. The woman in the glasses is Alla, our Moscow Intourist guide. The one in the checked shirt is "big" Natasha from the Friendship Society, who traveled with us and "mothered" us.

Vaulted ceiling inside the Faceted Hall, Moscow's most ancient municipal building, built 1487–1491.

view of the Moscow River (from
[K]remlin Cathedral).

We went into the apartment that Lenin lived in
for the last part of his life and saw his bedroom and
his study where his desk was still full of all his
personal books and pens and letter openers. They
keep everything just like it was when he died. Lenin
was the founder of the Soviet State. So he's sort of
like their George Washington.

Before we had dinner, we went to the American
embassy and talked to Ambassador Arthur Hartman.
(I thought the Ambassador might be strict, but he
was very nice and about as tall as my cousin Charlie.)
He said he hoped to see us again when we got back
from the Crimea on the Black Sea and our visit to
the Pioneer Camp at Artek. The Young Pioneers are
a little like Boy Scouts or Girl Scouts except that
their activities teach them about communism instead
of democracy.

The following day, we packed our swimsuits and flew hundreds of miles south to Simferopol in the Crimea, where it was warm and sunny. When I stepped off the plane, a bunch of Pioneers ran up with loads of flowers and they shouted my name and pulled me over to a special Artek minibus. They were very funny and giggly. They shouted, "Samanta! Samanta!" because there is no *th* sound in Russian. And I got to be very giggly, too. During the ride to Artek, we sang along with an accordion player, and the kids taught me several songs including a popular one in English:

> *May there always be sunshine,*
> *May there always be blue skies,*
> *May there always be mommy,*
> *May there always be me!*

When we arrived at Artek, a thousand children, who were all dressed in their Pioneer uniforms,

Greetings on our arrival at Artek.

started to sing songs of welcome. There was a band playing music and the Pioneers chanted my name. It all made me feel a little shy and speechless. Some teenaged dancers from the other side of the stadium came toward me carrying a round loaf of bread with a small bowl of salt sitting on top. Their dance looked like a scene from a ballet, and for a moment I felt like I was in a dream again.

The director of Artek introduced himself and asked if I wanted to stay with my parents or with Pioneer Girls at the Sea Camp dormitory. I didn't feel so shy now, so I said, "With the Pioneers!" The director introduced me to Olga, who was to be my section

The traditional bread and salt welcome. At first I didn't know if I was supposed to eat it or not. Finally I did and dipped the bread in the salt. It was delicious.

ISOO PO

leader, and off we went. They had a place ready at Sea Camp dormitory because there were more children in that section who knew a little English. Some of the ten girls in my room were Vera, Svieta, Illona, Vasilina, and Natasha Kashirina. Natasha and I became good friends right away. She was a little shy but she could speak English very well, mostly because her mother taught English at a school in Leningrad. Natasha is very beautiful and she is excellent at the piano and in ballet.

There was a balcony at the end of our dormitory room and, from my bed, I could look right out at the rocky beach and smell the salty Black Sea. It isn't really black or different from the Atlantic Ocean, except that there are no big waves and it's very salty. The extra saltiness makes it easier to float—it's almost like wearing a lifejacket when you're swimming around.

I thought Artek would be more rustic like nature camp or Girl Scout camp with tents and canoes, but it is much different. There are elegant gardens and winding roads everywhere that lead down to the sea, and there are almost four thousand kids from all over the Soviet Union. They were all very smart and talented. To get into Artek, you have to have super grades and also be an excellent musician, or be a genius in science, or a sports star, or know different languages. But everyone was very friendly and I never felt left out. I even made friends with some of the girls who couldn't speak English.

40

They gave me a blue-and-white visitor's scarf.

Olga and the girls in my room dressed me in an
Artek Pioneer uniform and tied my hair up with the
white chiffon bows that Soviet girls like to wear. I
wore the blue-and-white visitor's scarf because the
red one is only for regular members. When the time
came to get ready for bed, the girls acted just as silly
as I do, which was a relief, and then Olga said we
had to get to sleep and stop yakking. Even after Olga
turned the lights out, some of the girls whispered in
the dark. I wanted to whisper, too, but I was pooped
and fell asleep right away.

Artek is a very busy place. Everything is very
organized and the leaders and counselors are a big

Tanya and me.

Our days at Artek were also the final days of the Pioneers' camp session. The Neptune Festival, a water pageant, was part of their end-of-session activities.

help. It was near the end of the one-month session and all the kids were practicing their parts for the closing ceremonies. I was never so busy in my life.

One of the ceremonies was the Neptune Festival. There were swimming races and a water pageant and lots of clowning around. On the final day some of the Pioneer leaders were thrown into the water by their campers!

One day we went out on the Black Sea and threw bottles containing peace messages from the boat.

The kids had lots of questions about America—especially about clothes and music. They were all interested in how I lived and sometimes at night we talked about peace, but it didn't really seem necessary because none of them hated America, and none of them ever wanted war. Most of the kids had relatives or friends of their families die in World War II, and they hoped there would *never* be another war. It seemed strange even to talk about war when we all got along so well together. I guess that's what I came to find out. I mean, if we could be friends by just getting to know each other better, then what are our countries really arguing about? Nothing could be more important than *not* having a war if a war would kill everything. That's the way it seems to me.

On the second day, each Sea Camp kid wrote out a favorite wish for the future. We put the wishes in some old bottles and sealed them with corks and wax. Then we took an Artek boat out on the Black Sea and threw the bottles into the deep water. It was like the Black Sea was a wishing well. I wished for friendship and peace. There was a band on the boat, and we sang "May There Always Be Sunshine" and "Moskaya Dusha," which is about the soul of a sailor. We all linked arms and rocked back and forth while we sang. I sang a little in Russian, too.

On the third day at Artek, we drove along the coast of the Black Sea down to Yalta for a visit to Livadia Palace, where America and Russia had

Another activity was the championship swimming competition between the different Pioneer groups.

Natasha and me at the swimming
competition.

agreed to be friends and fight the Nazis in World War II. Natasha and some of the other Sea Campers came with us. Just when we were going into the meeting place, we met Mrs. Charles Schulz, whose husband draws *Peanuts*, standing outside. She was on a tour of the Soviet Union. She gave Natasha and me "Snoopy" pins to wear on our Pioneer uniforms. Inside the Yalta Palace, the director let me sit in President Roosevelt's chair at the famous meeting table. It was a huge chair and I tried to sit so my shoes would be flat on the floor and I wouldn't look like a little kid with dangling feet.

In the sunny Crimea during a driving tour of the coast.

We visited the Alupka Palace, the conference site at Yalta. I liked the lion.

A pensioner gave me an oil portrait
of myself that he had painted from
newspaper photos.

Singing "Moskaya Dusha."

"Artekevitch Sigda!" The Artek chant
meaning "Artek always!"

56

Our tour group at Yalta.

The Pioneers returned by boat from
Yalta to Artek.

We all danced at the closing
ceremonies.

My last night at Artek was the night of celebration for the end of the session, and there were parades and fireworks and dancing and costume shows. All the Pioneers were there and it lasted for hours. Even Mom and Dad were dancing. Some of the girls got to wear beautiful folk costumes for their dances and one group was all dressed in Misha-the-Bear outfits— a hundred dancing kids in Misha suits! It was the

There were almost a hundred kids
dancing in Misha costumes. Misha
the Bear was the symbol of the
Moscow Olympics in 1980.

biggest show ever. I gave a little speech and said goodbye to everybody.

My parents went to a dinner party next door to the Artek Hotel where they were staying. And Natasha and I got permission to sleep at the hotel that night. But we were too excited to do much sleeping. We got up and dressed around midnight and sneaked over to the party to get some cake and soda. The camp director was there and he said that Natasha could go to the airport with us the next

Our farewell song. This was a little sad because we were leaving the next day.

Last view of Artek and the Black Sea, including the "Twin Sisters" rocks.

Saying goodbye from the Artek bus.

day, which we thought was a great idea, and we promised to go to bed.

We only slept for about five hours because we wanted to get up early and visit a state collective farm before I flew to Leningrad with my parents. A collective farm is owned by the Soviet government. It has its own little community of people who live in one area and work on the surrounding farm.

The collective farm family invited us to lunch before we left for Leningrad.

The fruit at the collective farm was delicious.

The state farm was like a small town. Three thousand people live there and work on the farm or go to school. The directors of the farm did experiments on fruit, and they had a table set up out in the middle of an orchard with bowls of absolutely giant fruit—raspberries the size of Ping-Pong balls, for instance. Natasha and I played in the orchard and picked peaches right off the trees. Then we had a huge lunch at a farm superintendent's home with his wife and sons and grandchildren.

Back at the Simferopol Airport, I felt pretty sad when the plane started its engines, but I didn't cry because Natasha and I had planned to meet again in Leningrad in a few days.

Leningrad is full of ancient palaces, which I like better than modern skyscrapers. The city was bombed by the Nazis in World War II for almost three years and lots of people starved to death. Almost one-half million people died there, and now there are monuments and cemeteries everywhere. We left flowers at many of these places, and then went to our hotel to rest.

The Kirov Ballet in Leningrad is all blue and gold inside, and probably the most beautiful place I've ever seen.

On our second night in Leningrad, Gennady and "big" Natasha took us to the famous Kirov Ballet, whose special building is all blue and gold inside and probably the most beautiful place I've ever seen. We saw *The Fountains of Bakhchisaray* ballet and Alla Cizova was the prima ballerina. When the first act ended, we went out and a guide showed us backstage where the dancers were getting ready for the next part of the performance. I could hardly see anything—it was so dark. Then Alla Cizova ran up to us and she presented me with a pair of her toe shoes.

We saw *The Fountains of Bakhchisaray* ballet, and Alla Cizova, the prima ballerina, gave me a pair of toe shoes.

She signed her autograph on them and said something in Russian and then had to run back to get ready. We went to our seats again and the lights dimmed down and the next act started. I could hardly watch the show because I was trying to get the toe shoes on. Mom made me stop, so after the next act I went over to sit with "big" Natasha and she let me sneak the toe shoes on and I tied the ribbons around my ankles. They fit! Alla Cizova and I were the same size! It's a good thing I have big feet for my age.

Our Intourist guide explains that the sign says "900 Days," referring to the Siege of Leningrad.

Monument to the Heroic Defenders of Leningrad. During the 900-day siege by the Nazis, one-half million Soviets died.

Museum at Piskarevskoye cemetery. During the 900-day siege, a young girl named Galia Savicheva kept a diary noting the dates her relatives died. Eventually she died as well.

Leningrad has "white nights" in the summertime because it's close to the North Pole. We left the Kirov Ballet about eleven o'clock at night and the sun was just starting to go down. I had trouble sleeping until it finally got dark. Maybe the people of Leningrad enjoy the extra daylight. Back at our hotel there were crowds of young people joking around on the sidewalk and singing songs after midnight.

The statue of Lenin in front of the Smolny, headquarters for the October Revolution. I'm walking with "big" Natasha, Helen, our Intourist guide, and Vera from the Leningrad Friendship Society.

Tomb of the Unknown Soldier at
Piskarevskoye.

The *Aurora* is the ship that gave the signal that started the Russian Revolution. The *Aurora* is now a museum.

A sailor on the *Aurora* gave me flowers and a china polar bear, the symbol of the *Aurora*.

Mom and me and "little" Natasha waiting for the fountains at Tsar Peter's Summer Palace to get going.

On our last day in Leningrad, "little" Natasha and her mother joined us for a hydrofoil boatride to Tsar Peter's Summer Palace on the Gulf of Finland. After a tour of the Palace and its beautiful fountains and gardens, we went back to our hotel for lunch and tea. I got Natasha to try on my Cizova ballet shoes. (We had traded shoes all the time back in Artek.) She could stand right up on her toes without holding on to a chair. It hurt like crazy when I tried

Some of the fountains are tricky—
you have to run in and out when
the water stops for a second.

The fountains at Tsar Peter's Summer Palace.

it. Then we went downstairs and played a duet on an incredible gold-trimmed piano we found on the second floor. We played everything we knew several times over because Natasha had to go home at the end of the afternoon. I wished we could have just played on and on.

Late in the afternoon, we visited Tsar Peter's Winter Palace, which is now the famous Hermitage Museum. Natasha had been there before, many times. We only had enough time to see a few of the rooms. Someone said that a tour of the Hermitage would last six years if you spent one minute looking at each work of art. When we left the museum, after a sad goodbye, Natasha and her mother headed home.

Natasha and I tried on the toe shoes
from Alla Cizova in our room at the
hotel.

86

Looking across Revolution Square toward the Winter Palace, the Hermitage.

Meeting with Leningrad schoolchildren at the Leningrad Pioneer Palace—a real palace given to the Pioneers. It is also called the House of Peace and Friendship.

Vera Brovkina from the Leningrad Friendship Society had a dinner party for us the night we left to return to Moscow. Everybody at the party was making toasts, which the Soviets love to do, and so I tried one, too. With my wineglass of Pepsi, I toasted Scotty and Matthew, the cameramen from Maine, who had to carry their own battery packs and once stumbled and fell down trying to walk backwards ahead of us with their cameras. We were going to take the midnight train to Moscow. It was a sleeper train called the "Red Arrow Express."

At the train station, the conductor wore a uniform like a stewardess, and she showed us the compartments with the pull-down beds and then made Russian tea for everybody in a big samovar. "Big" Natasha and I had a compartment together and I fell asleep right away when the train started going clickety-clack.

Madame Tereshkova went into space almost twenty years ago. Now she is director of the Soviet Women's Committee, a very important job in the Soviet Union.

It seemed funny to be back in Moscow again. It felt like we'd been gone for months but it was really only a week. Ambassador and Mrs. Hartman sent a message to the hotel inviting us to their private home, Spasso House, for lunch the next day, which was a great treat because they had hamburgers and french fries and everything. It was just like being back in America suddenly. He and his wife were very friendly and acted like neighbors.

And the next day we went to the Soviet Women's Committee for our luncheon appointment with Madame Tereshkova. She hugged me to pieces and we talked about how dangerous it is to have our countries afraid of each other and spending so much money on war equipment. She hoped our countries could be friends once again and spend our time and money on peaceful activities. I think she was very thoughtful about the importance of friendship. Maybe someday

Resting before the fountains start up at the Exhibition of Economic Achievements in Moscow.

she'll be the first woman president of the Soviet Union.

The next afternoon, Mom and I toured some of the Moscow subway stations with "big" Natasha, and it was amazing to see chandeliers down there, and the whole place looks like an underground palace or something you might see in an old movie. They actually use it for a regular subway. The escalators to the subway are really long and steep and faster

The Bolshoi Ballet was closed for
repairs, but the director let us in for
a peek. It's beautiful red velvet and
gold inside.

than ours. I don't know how older people manage to use them.

The Bolshoi Ballet was closed for repairs, but we went over one afternoon and the assistant director showed us around. In Moscow, the people say the Bolshoi is the world's best, and in Leningrad they say the Kirov is best. They also say the same things about their subways!

During the rest of our stay in Moscow, we were always on the go. We visited the Krylatskoye Olympic Center, where I tried out a racing bicycle in the Velodrome and got a lesson from some Soviet gymnasts.

ГОСТИНИЦА
"СОВЕТСКАЯ"

am standing with one of the Moscow policemen who helped us get around the city in a hurry.

The Krylatskoye Olympic Center,
looking down on the Velodrome.

At the Moscow Olympic Center they
let me ride a racing bicycle. It was
way too big for me, so expert cyclists
rode beside me, just in case.

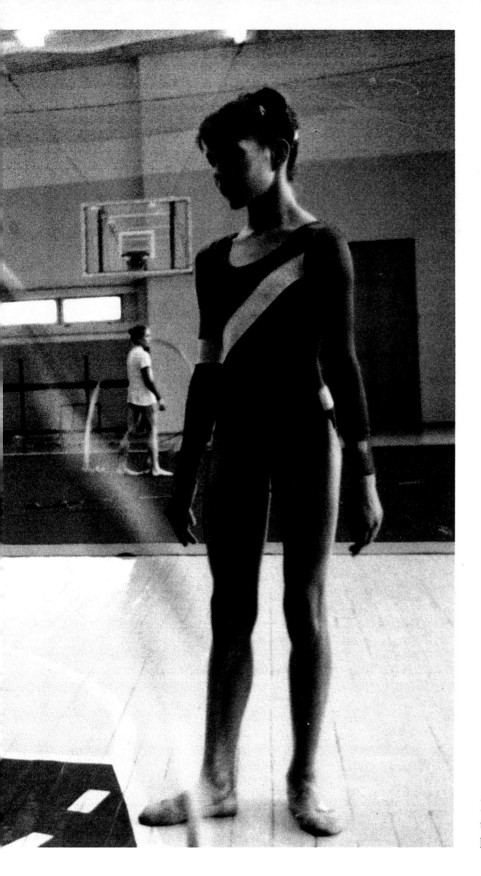

In another part of the Olympic Center, champion gymnasts showed me how to twirl ribbons.

I had only had a year of gymnastics
lessons when I was younger, so I
needed lots of help.

The Moscow Circus is one of the most famous in the world. It was jammed with people from all over— one man two rows in front of us stood up and shouted, "Hi, Samantha! I'm from California!"

We also went to the famous Moscow Circus, where a performer drew a caricature of me. We saw other performances at Natalia Durova's Animal Theater and the Moscow Puppet Theater. And during a side trip to the city of Zagorsk, we spent an afternoon at the Toy Museum.

Natalia Durova's Animal Theater.

This caricature of me was drawn by
a member of the circus.

We visited the Puppet Theater in
Moscow, where there are daily shows
and exhibits.

During a side trip from Moscow we
visited the Toy Museum in Zagorsk.

A *matrioshka* (nesting doll) at the
Toy Museum.

On our next to last day in Moscow, Madame Krouglova had a sort of farewell luncheon for us at the Friendship Society headquarters in a huge room with waiters and everything. I wore my folk costume with the pearl headdress (called *kokoshnik*) that the Moscow Pioneer children made for me. Madame Krouglova gave me one of her powerful hugs and she didn't even get annoyed when I found a piano in the corner of the room and played it instead of politely staying at the table. The Soviets love kids so much that I might be spoiled if I lived there.

On our last full day in Moscow, Gennady and Natasha found out that Mr. Andropov was still very busy with his government work but he promised to send his deputy and some other Kremlin officials over to the hotel to have a meeting with us. The hotel staff fixed up the dining room in our suite with extra chairs and piled all sorts of fruit and snacks on the table. The Kremlin deputy who came over was Mr. Leonid Zamyatin. He had white hair and

Each town or area has a Pioneer
meeting place. The large ones are
called Pioneer Palaces. In Moscow
the Central Pioneer Palace is a large,
modern building.

Children danced for us at the Moscow Pioneer Palace.

This little boy is a great a cappella singer with a loud and beautiful voice.

looked like a businessman from America. He and his friends were all sort of formal but very nice. He said that Mr. Andropov sent his apology for not being able to see us. We talked about how our countries needed to be friends and how my trip might help that come true. Gennady did the translating between us, but I think Mr. Zamyatin knows English. A couple of times he interrupted Gennady's translation and changed the words. One of the waiters was serving Russian tea to everybody, and he was so nervous that the teacups rattled like crazy when he carried them to the table. I was staring at the waiter because it was funny, but I didn't laugh. I don't think he was nervous about me.

Then Mr. Zamyatin's helpers brought in some gifts that Mr. Andropov sent over. There was a real Russian samovar, and a fancy teapot, and a lacquered wooden box (a *palech*) that had a painting of Red Square on the top. The gifts were really beautiful and each one came with Mr. Andropov's actual

calling card. Our gift to Mr. Andropov was from the whole family. It was a book of all of Mark Twain's speeches—*Mark Twain Speaking*. We thought Mr. Andropov might like it because we knew he liked Mr. Twain's stories, and Mr. Andropov also had to make speeches. Pretty soon we were all saying goodbye and shaking hands and Mr. Zamyatin and his friends got ready to go. This was our last official meeting and it meant that our trip was really almost over.

In the morning, we said goodbye to everyone at a press conference in Moscow and then went to Sheremetjevo Airport and hugged all of our new friends for the last time.

On our return flight, we had to stop in Gander, Newfoundland, Montreal, and Boston. There were reporters and camera crews everywhere. I was quite tired by now and not very talkative. I was just ready to get back to Maine and our home. The next day, I got to ride in a convertible during the Manchester

Our final press conference in the Moscow hotel the morning we left.

Festival, and Governor Brennan was there, along with most of my friends. The whole day was just perfect because it made me feel that I was really home again. I think Maine is a good place to come home to.

It's hard to believe how lucky I've been and how much my life was changed by writing that letter. The world seems not so complicated as it did when I looked at travel books from the library. And the people of the world seem more like people in my own neighborhood. I think they are more like me than I ever realized. I guess that's the most important change inside me.

Sometimes I still worry that the next day will be the last day of the Earth. But with more people thinking about the problems of the world, I hope that someday soon we will find the way to world peace. Maybe someone will show us the way.

Home again!